A MERMAID GIRL

By Sana Rafi

Illustrated by Olivia Aserr

VIKING

Mama and I are mermaid girls.
When we dip our bodies in the water,
our worries float away.

We enjoy its rhythm and ripples,
reminiscing about the other
mermaid girls
who aren't here with us.

Today is an extra-special day.

"Are you ready to sparkle, my little mermaid girl?" asks Mama.

"You, little lady, are going to shimmer and glisten in your new suit."

When I put it on, I feel like
a dainty seahorse,

or a splendid pineapplefish!

My burkini makes me feel
like I can do anything.

Mama puts on her matching swimsuit.

"We're twins!" I exclaim.
"Like two lighthouses-people can
spot us from afar," says Mama.

"Your burkini tells a powerful
story of who you are. You
look dazzling, little star.

Now remember, always keep your
head tipped up to the sun . . ."

I'm going to swirl and flip my mermaid tail!
And fly like a sea butterfly!

Mama takes pictures of this day for
the faraway mermaid girls.
I smile big.

Soon, we arrive at the blue-white zigzagging pool.

"Will you be able to *swim* in that?" asks Sam.
"Yes!" I announce proudly.
"My new swimsuit is awesome!"

"But it doesn't look like a real swimsuit," Angie says simply.

"That's not true," I whisper.
But when I look around, I see they're right.

I don't fit in.

"I'm standing out too much." My lips tremble.
Mama puts a hand on my shoulder.
"Sometimes, to stand out is to be full of courage.
Full of all the things that make you, you."

She reminds me of all the brave
mermaid girls who came before me.
"Long before us, your grandmother
and her grandmother razzle-dazzled
in their burkinis just as colorful as yours.
Many more will come after you.

You are not alone."

Mama's right.
So I take a deep breath
and stride toward the
diving board.

I jump, giving the sky a big high five.

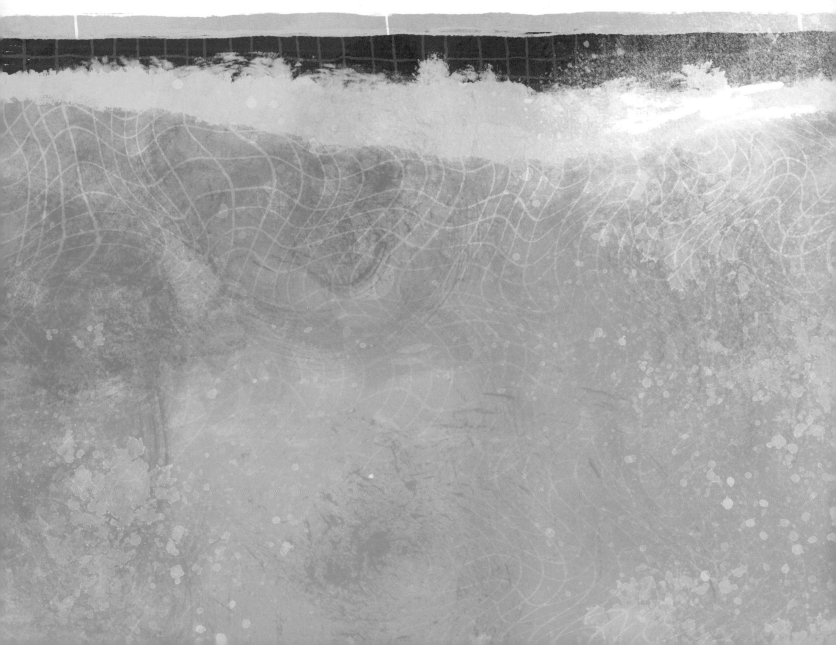

"Wow!" Sam says.
      "Watch me too!"

Next, we toss coins.
My burkini shines like a yellow gemstone.

"Can you splash dance in your new
swimsuit just like us?" asks Sam.
Of course I can!

"Can you play Submarine Race in your new swimsuit just like us?" asks Angie.

Of course I can!

Together, we line up against the wall.
"On your mark! Get set! Go!"
We set off toward the deep end as fast as we can.

My swimsuit hugs me as we
pretend to be deep sea creatures.
I sing under the soundless water
and do headstands like an upside-
down jellyfish!

Now my friends know my
swimsuit is a real swimsuit.
"You're like a mermaid girl,"
they say.
"Can we be mermaid girls too?"
Sam and Angie ask.

We hold hands and swim to the bottom,
twisting our bodies.

We twinkle like our ancestor mermaids.
We beam at ourselves for who we are becoming.
We blaze ahead,

leaving our glimmer for all the mermaid girls to come.

For Zeyb and Zayan, my dazzling little stars.
Always be true to your story. —S. R.

For my parents,
who taught me to be a mermaid. —O. A.

VIKING
An imprint of Penguin Random House LLC, New York

First published in the United States of America by Viking,
an imprint of Penguin Random House LLC, 2022

Text copyright © 2022 by Sana Rafi
Illustrations copyright © 2022 by Olivia Aserr

Visit us online at penguinrandomhouse.com.

Library of Congress Cataloging-in-Publication Data is available.

Manufactured in China

ISBN 9780593327609

1 3 5 7 9 10 8 6 4 2

HH

Design by Lucia Baez • Text set in Seven Seas

The art for this book was created digitally.